TITLE: Trackside

Written by: Collin Anderson

CHAPTER ONE –

Liam had always believed in noise. As a kid, it meant life. The sound of tires in gravel, the click of a chain on a garage door, his mom yelling through drywall — all of it meant the world was still turning. But these days, it was the quiet that told him everything was okay.

His house was quiet now. Dinner dishes done. Jessica upstairs with Penelope, reading the same book for the third time. Riley in her room, earbuds in, writing lyrics or poetry or whatever it was sixteen-year-olds poured themselves into when they didn't know what else to do with how they felt. Liam stood barefoot in the garage, hand resting on a polished frame, one overhead light buzzing above.

Jack's bike sat in Bay Two. Pristine. Finished. Never ridden.

He kept it clean — out of respect, maybe. Out of guilt, definitely. Jack had been out for two years now. He had a wife. A kid. A home of his own just twenty minutes away. But the bay was still Jack's. Liam never put another bike there. Never hung tools above it. Just kept it waiting.

The garage had three bays: one for Liam's current project, one for Jack's ghost, and one for the dream they never got to build — a customer bay, where young riders would come in, learn the trade, shoot the shit, and ride out better men. That last bay had a cracked concrete floor and no power tools. He kept it that way. A reminder.

He pulled a tarp off the workbench, revealing an old photo — sun-bleached, oil-stained. Two kids on a rusted-out Yamaha, helmets too big for their heads, grinning like they hadn't seen the world yet. Jack was flipping off the camera. Liam was laughing too hard to care.

The garage door creaked behind him.

Jessica stood there, arms folded, her hair tied back, eyes soft.

"You coming to bed?" she asked.

"In a bit," Liam said, wiping his hands on a shop towel.

She walked in and looked at the bike.

"You think he'll ever ride it?" she asked.

Liam didn't answer for a while. Just looked at the seat, the grip tape Jack liked, and the tiny skull valve caps Riley bought him on his first Father's Day out.

"He might," Liam said.

Jessica stepped closer. Slid an arm around his waist.

"You miss him?" she asked.

"He's not gone."

"That's not what I asked."

Liam sighed.

"Yeah. I do."

She leaned into him.

"He's not yours to carry, you know."

Liam kissed the top of her head.

"I know," he said. "But some things just stick."

They stood there for a long time. The garage buzzing. The smell of old gas. The photo still sitting out on the bench.

Liam thought about calling Jack. Thought about inviting him over. He didn't. He just turned off the light and followed Jessica back into the quiet.

Behind them, the garage door hummed shut. Bay Two stayed dark. But clean.

Waiting.

Just waiting.

The trains ran past their neighborhood like a warning.

Big freights, slow and loud, the kind that rattled windows and shook loose the rust from porch railings. Liam used to lie awake at night and listen to them moan through the dark, a constant reminder of everything that was leaving town — and everything that never would.

They grew up on the trackside. Not the good side. Not even the bad side. Just the forgotten stretch of cracked roads and broken fences where nobody looked twice.

If you lived trackside, you learned early that nothing was coming for you. Not help. Not luck. Not a future. Only noise — the endless clatter of someone else's life passing you by.

Liam met Jack out there, back when they were just angry boys with cut-up sneakers and too much time. Jack had a busted-up dirt bike and a cigarette behind his ear.

Liam had scraped knuckles and a chip on his shoulder the size of the town itself.

They were brothers from the start. Not by blood — by survival.

Jack had a father who loved his bike more than his kid.

Liam had a mother who loved him but ran out of ways to show it after too many long nights and too many overdue bills.

The two of them found each other in the middle of it — on cracked sidewalks, in alleys behind shuttered stores, down by the dead-end where the tracks split the town like an old scar nobody bothered to stitch up.

That was the thing about growing up trackside.

You learned how to take a hit.

You learned how to throw one back.

They weren't brothers by blood. They were brothers by necessity. Two angry boys growing up on the trackside, trying to be bigger than the hand they were dealt.

But even angry boys find reasons to hope sometimes. Even if they don't last.

Jessica came into Liam's life on a Tuesday. Liam was freshly 20 and living his life wide open.

He was fixing a busted tail light outside Manny's Garage, sweat running into his eyes, cursing the heat and his hands and everything else he couldn't fix.

She was just there — dropping off her sister's car, laughing into the sun like she didn't know places like this were supposed to kill people's dreams.

Jessica didn't ask Liam where he came from. She didn't ask why he looked at the ground when he talked, or why he never said more than he had to.

She just smiled like she already knew him. And for the first time in a long time, Liam didn't feel like he had to run.

Jack met Shannon the way Jack met most things: headfirst.

She was tending bar at O'Malley's on a night when the air was too thick and Jack's fists were itching for a fight. It was his 21st and he wasn't leaving without a story.

She didn't flinch when he barked orders. Didn't giggle at his bad jokes.

She just stared him down like she wasn't impressed — and Jack, for once, didn't know what the hell to do with himself.

Shannon called him on his bullshit before he ever got the chance to feed her a lie.

And Jack, who had spent most of his life building armor so thick no one could see through it, let her inside without a second thought.

Maybe that's why he loved her. Maybe that's why he never could figure out how to keep her safe from the war inside his own head.

CHAPTER TWO –

He woke before the lights came on. He always did.

The cell was cold, but not in a way he noticed anymore. It had long since soaked into his bones and settled into the muscle. The kind of cold that wasn't about temperature. The kind that came from concrete and silence.

Jack sat up on the lower bunk, feet on the floor. His cellmate, some kid who'd probably be gone in six months, still snored above him. Jack didn't know his name. Didn't care to. People came and went. Time didn't.

He cracked his knuckles one at a time, slow and quiet. Routine. Then he stood, stretched, and started his day like he had for the last eight years — with control. Because in here, control was currency. And chaos was death.

The door slid open at six. He stepped out without looking back.

The yard was gray and wide and already humming. Men moving in tight cliques. Conversations that looked casual but weren't. Deals, tensions, and warnings passed in glances. Jack walked through it all untouched.

He didn't run the place. Not officially. But people moved when he moved.

At the far end of the yard, by the fence with the bent post, he sat on the same bench he always did. Facing the same cracked section of wall. He didn't watch the men. He listened.

There was a rhythm in prison. Not the one the guards tried to keep. A deeper one. The pace of survival. You learned it, or you didn't last long.

"Jack," someone said, a voice behind him.

He didn't turn.

"New guy wants to speak to you."

Still didn't turn.

"Tell him to speak when he's ready to speak for himself."

The messenger lingered. Then walked away.

Jack exhaled through his nose and watched a bird hop across the yard fence — a busted wing, probably clipped trying to land. It flapped once, twice, then fell. Still tried to move.

He respected that. Sometimes he felt like the bird. Sometimes whatever clipped it.

Inside, the clocks didn't tick. But Jack kept time anyway. One hour of reading. Two meals. Thirty minutes of workout. One letter from Shannon every Friday. If it didn't come, he didn't ask why. But when it did — he read it slow, twice.

He had a box of them under his bunk. Twelve years' worth. Everyone signed, "Still here. – S."

They talked about nothing: the weather, a new recipe, a memory from when they were kids. But Jack remembered each one like a map. Like it was the only thing that kept him from disappearing completely.

There was no freedom in prison. But there were anchors. And Shannon had been his.

That night, back in the cell, Jack lay on his bunk staring at the ceiling. His cellmate was coughing in his sleep. Someone two tiers over was screaming about a bad dream. He could hear every step of the guards as it echoed in the cellblock.

Jack didn't move.

He just stared up at the cracked paint above his bed — and whispered, just once:

"I'm still here too."

CHAPTER THREE –

They met over motor oil and busted exhaust.

Liam was twelve. Jack was thirteen. Both of them already knew more about two-stroke engines than their teachers knew about algebra. That's how it was in neighborhoods like theirs — where the streets were cracked and the houses leaned just a little too far forward like they were eavesdropping on the lives inside.

Jack's uncle ran a bike chop behind a liquor store, half-legal and fully sacred. Liam used to ride by on his pushbike just to listen. The clank of sockets, the low rumble of an idling twin — that was church. One day he stopped and leaned against the fence for hours until someone finally barked, "You gonna stand there or you gonna sweep?"

Jack was the one who handed him the broom.

Didn't say a word. Just nodded toward the pile of rusted bolts in the corner. Liam swept. Jack handed him a rag. They didn't speak much that first day at the shop. They didn't need to.

Some friendships start loud. This one started with grease and silence.

By fourteen, they were rebuilding a salvaged Yamaha from parts they couldn't afford and tools that barely worked. They'd sneak out at night, roll the frame down the driveway to keep the noise down and work under a broken security light in Liam's garage, drinking flat soda and talking about engines like poets.

It was Jack who said it first.

"We start a club one day. Just us. Then we build it."

Liam nodded, eyes on a spark plug.

"What would we call it?"

Jack didn't even blink. "Out of towners."

Liam looked up. "Why?"

"Because no one gives a shit about towns like this," Jack said. "And if we're gonna ride outta here, we're taking our name with us."

They made patches out of denim scraps. Drew the logo in a school notebook. Rode beat-up dirt bikes through alleys like they were tailing ghosts.

It wasn't about crime. Not yet. It was about speed. About belonging. About two kids who didn't fit in anywhere — except on a bike, with each other.

They got into fights. With older kids, with teachers, with anyone who looked at them like they were trash. Jack hit harder. Liam hit smarter. They never lost when they were together.

Some nights they'd ride out to the edge of the freeway and just sit there, helmets off, watching taillights disappear into the distance.

"That's gonna be us," Jack said once, pointing at the horizon. "One day we ride and don't come back."

Liam looked at him, then down at the oil on his hands.

"Promise me we don't do it stupid."

Jack smirked.

"I don't do anything stupid."

Liam threw an oil-soaked rag at him. They laughed so hard they cried.

Back then, the road felt endless, friendship felt eternal, and they felt bulletproof.

They didn't know yet that some promises don't break loud. They just *fade.*

CHAPTER FOUR –

They weren't trying to be criminals.

Not at first.

It was supposed to be a test — something stupid and fast, just to prove they weren't the kind of guys who lived and died on the same four blocks like their uncles and fathers before them.

Jack still remembered the rush. It was a high he couldn't forget.

They were sixteen. There was a liquor store two towns over, tucked under a freeway ramp. The owner was old, tired. Kept the register in plain view and left the front door unlocked after dark. They'd been watching for weeks. Riding past. Timing shifts. Reading rhythms like a song.

It wasn't about the money.

It was about control.

Jack sat on the curb outside Liam's garage, lacing up the same boots he'd worn to school that morning. His heart wasn't pounding. He felt calm. Clean.

Liam came out carrying a duffel bag. Flashlight. Gloves. Two bandanas.

"You sure?" Liam asked.

Jack nodded once.

"Of course." He said, sounding more like a seasoned pro than a first-timer.

The ride there was quiet. They took the back roads. No music. Just the hum of engines and the occasional crackle of gravel under rubber. The night air was cool, and the streets were empty in that way only suburbs know how to be — like they're holding their breath.

They parked a block away. Walked the last hundred yards. Jack led. Liam carried the bag.

Inside, it went fast.

Jack hopped the counter while Liam kept his eyes on the door. The old man never even looked up. Jack pulled the drawer and stuffed the bills into his jacket. No threats. No shouting. No gun.

And then it was over.

They ran. Back to the bikes. Gone in less than three minutes.

Back at the garage, they dumped the money on a tarp — sweaty bills, maybe two hundred dollars.

Liam looked at it like it might burn him.

Jack had a different reaction.

"That's it?" asked Liam.

Jack didn't answer. He was staring at his hands. They weren't shaking. He wanted them to be. But they weren't.

Liam finally sat down.

"That's it," Jack said. "That's the first time we've ever done a job together. A real deal job."

Liam didn't smile.

"Does it feel like winning?" he asked.

Jack shrugged. "Feels like breathing."

They didn't spend the money.

Jack kept his cut in a tin box under his bed for years.

Not because he was proud of it.

Because that was the night they crossed a line — and never looked back.

Liam didn't know it yet but that night would rewrite his story in ways he couldn't comprehend. I

CHAPTER FIVE –

Jack's house was the kind of place where the TV was always on and nobody watched it.

Cigarette smoke in the walls. Ashtrays on the floor. A Harley frame was stripped bare in the middle of the living room like furniture.

His dad didn't speak much. When he did, it was in instructions. Or curses. Sometimes both.

Jack's father loved his Harley more than anything else in the world.

The chrome got polished. The tires got replaced. The engine got tuned by hand every Sunday.

Jack didn't get much of anything.

He learned early that machines were easier to fix than people — and a lot harder to disappoint.

Maybe that's why he spent so much time trackside, tinkering with bikes no one else wanted, building something that couldn't leave him when it got bored.

Jack never talked about it.

He didn't have to.

Liam saw it in the way he flinched at loud doors. In the way, he shut down when someone yelled without warning. He wasn't scared, just *prepared*.

Liam saw it most In the way Jack held silence like a shield.

Liam's house wasn't like that.

His mom was love and fury wrapped in the same breath. She worked doubles at the law firm, raised two kids alone, and kept a shotgun under the sink just in case.

She'd scream if Liam came home late — then cry while patching the scrape on his knee.

She made him the man of the house and he had no choice in it.

Different worlds.

But both of them knew what it meant to feel small.

Unheard.

Unseen.

They found each other in the alley behind the corner store. Thirteen years old. Jack had a busted knuckle. Liam had a black eye from a school fight. They sat on milk crates and said nothing for a long time.

Then Jack said: "You ever just wanna break something?"

Liam nodded. "Every day."

That was the beginning.

They built bikes out of trash. Raced them down hills until the brakes gave out. Jack skinned his elbow once so bad it tore through his shirt. He didn't even flinch. Liam was the one who cleaned it and poured peroxide over the wound while Jack hissed through gritted teeth.

"Don't be soft," Jack muttered.

"I'm not," Liam said. "But you don't gotta bleed for nothing."

They didn't talk about feelings. They talked about engines, chrome, and the smell of gasoline.

But it was love. The kind that didn't need to be said.

At fifteen, they got matching reaper tattoos on their arms — half-joking, half-oath.

One night, Jack's dad kicked him out for "running his mouth."

He showed up at Liam's door with a backpack and a busted lip.

Liam's mom didn't say anything. Just made up the couch and left out an extra plate at dinner.

They were truly brothers after that.

No questions. No ceremony. Just a choice.

One summer night, they rode out to the hills — the place where the streetlights ended and the stars started.

They sat in the dirt beside their bikes, staring up at the sky like it held something better.

"You think we make it out?" Liam asked.

Jack didn't answer right away. Then:

"No. But I think we can be remembered. I think we can make it all worth something"

Liam didn't forget that.

Not when the engines blew.

Not when the cops showed up.

Not when the blood hit the concrete.

And not when Jack started slipping into a version of himself Liam didn't recognize.

CHAPTER SIX –

It wasn't supposed to be a real job.

Just a favor.

A quick grab.

Something Shane had lined up with one of his dirtbag friends who worked nights at a pawn shop in Riverside. In and out. No heat. No drama.

Shane was Jack's older cousin, he was what you might consider the cool older guy. he'd been to jail before, and he rode motorcycles and seemed to be everything Jack and Liam dreamed of.

Just one problem, Shane was dumb, really dumb, and way too nervous.

Jack brought Liam because that's what he always did.

They drove out past midnight. Shane was behind the wheel, twitchy and grinning, talking fast and wild like he'd already pulled it off. Jack sat in the passenger seat, quiet. Watching. Liam sat in the back with the duffel bag, eyeing the crowbar Shane insisted they bring.

The plan was simple:

Shane's guy left the back door propped.

They slip in, grab the cash from the safe, and maybe a couple small pieces they could fence easy — watches, rings, no guns.

Fifteen minutes, tops.

But from the second they stepped inside, it felt wrong.

The air was stale. The lights too bright. The safe wasn't where Shane said it'd be. And there were **two guys** working — not one.

One of them wasn't supposed to be there.

He had a shotgun. And he wasn't bluffing.

Shane panicked first.

Grabbed a display case and hurled it.

Glass shattered.

The guy with the gun fired once — into the ceiling — but it was enough.

Jack tackled him.

Liam screamed his name.

Shane was already grabbing a box of watches and kicking open drawers like he didn't even hear the shot.

It all spiraled from there.

Liam tried to pull Jack off the guy.

Shane was yelling, "Get the fuckin' cash!"

The second worker — a kid, maybe twenty — grabbed a pipe from behind the counter and came swinging.

Jack elbowed him in the face. Hard.

The kid dropped. Didn't move.

Jack kicked him on the ground.

Poor kid was out cold. Probably worse.

Liam froze.

This wasn't just theft anymore.

It was assault.

It was blood on tile.

It was a gun on the ground and a siren in the distance.

It was too late.

"Go!" Jack shouted, grabbing Liam's jacket.

They bolted out the back. Shane dropped half the haul trying to fit it into the duffel. Jack shoved him into the car. Liam slammed the door.

Nobody spoke for ten minutes.

They parked in an empty lot near the rail yard. Shane lit a cigarette with bloody knuckles, hands shaking.

"Did you see that guy's face?" he said, laughing. "You dropped him, Jack. You dropped him like a fuckin' movie."

Jack didn't answer.

He was staring at his hands.

There was blood on his sleeve. Not his.

Liam leaned forward between the seats.

"You said it'd be easy."

Shane snorted. "It was."

Liam's voice dropped.

"We might've killed someone."

Shane just shrugged. "We didn't."

Jack spoke then. Quiet.

"But we might've."

Silence.

That was the first time Liam looked at Jack and didn't recognize him.

Eyes wide. Hands still.

Like he was **calm** in the aftermath.

And Liam knew.

This wasn't the end of something.

It was the start.

CHAPTER SEVEN –

They didn't speak for three days after the pawn shop job.

Liam spent most of that time in the garage, hands deep in a rebuild he didn't care about. Just needed to keep them moving. Jack hadn't called. Shane had, once. Left a voicemail like it was all just another wild night.

But Liam couldn't shake it.

The blood. The kid's face. The way Jack had smiled afterward — not big, not wild, but that low, quiet grin. Like it had clicked. Like it was where he belonged.

Jessica had started looking at Liam differently. Like she could see the road he was heading down even when he couldn't.

Shannon, too. She didn't beg Jack to stop. That wasn't her way. She just stayed quieter, stayed later behind the bar, stopped asking him if he'd be home for dinner.

They met at the old shop behind Shane's uncle's place. Neutral ground. Cement walls, cracked windows, smell of old oil. The kind of place where secrets soaked into the floor.

Jack leaned against a workbench, eating sunflower seeds, calm like nothing happened.

Liam shoved his hands into his jacket pockets, feeling the sweat cool on his skin, the nausea curling in his gut.

"You think this is it?" Liam muttered. "Running outta back doors with cash flying everywhere? You think this is the life we bled for?"

Jack chuckled under his breath, a sick kind of joy still twitching at the corners of his mouth.

"Better than starving," Jack said.

Liam stepped in closer, voice low. "Better than starving ain't the same as better than dying, Jack. You don't even see it, do you? You're trying to outrun the grave and you're dragging me with you."

Jack wiped his nose on the sleeve of his jacket, that wired, reckless look still burning in his eyes.

"We got out. Ain't that what you wanted? Outta that dead town? Outta those broken houses?"

Liam shook his head slowly. "Not like this."

For a second, Jack just stared at him — and there was something hollow there, something already halfway gone.

"This is all I know how to be," Jack said finally, voice rough. "I'm good at running. Good at swinging. Good at surviving. You want a better man? He died trackside before we ever knew his name." He growled

"You get some sleep?" Jack asked.

Liam stood near the doorway. Didn't move in. Anger building up inside.

"We killed someone, Jack."

Jack spit a shell into a can. " WE didn't," he emphasized.

Liam stepped closer, jaw tight.

"That's not the point."

Jack looked at him then — really looked. Saw the twitch in his eye. The coil in his shoulders.

"You're rattled."

"I'm awake." Liam hissed through clenched teeth.

Jack shrugged. "You always knew what this was."

"No," Liam said. "I knew what *we* were. Two kids with bikes and broken homes, trying to outrun whatever shit we were born into. But this?" He gestured around them, the oil-stained floor, the duffel bag half full of stolen gear. "This wasn't the dream."

Jack pushed off the bench.

"It's not a dream anymore. It's real. We're in it. We made it work. You want out now?"

Liam stepped up, face to face.

"I want to breathe again. I want to look in the mirror and not wonder who I'm turning into."

Jack shook his head. "You sound like someone who forgot where we came from."

"No," Liam said. "I sound like someone who finally sees where we're headed."

Silence.

Jack broke it. Voice low.

"So what? You done?"

Liam looked down. Then back up.

"I don't know. But I can't keep following you into fires like it's the only way to stay close. I keep getting burned."

Jack's eyes narrowed.

"You think you're better than me now?"

"No," Liam said. "I think I'm scared of who we're becoming."

That landed.

Jack didn't yell. Didn't argue.

He just stepped back, picked up the can of seeds, and tossed it in the trash.

Then, without looking at Liam:

"You were the only one who ever saw me. Don't start looking away now."

Liam didn't move. Didn't speak.

The air between them wasn't angry. It was heavier than that.

It was tired. It was soaked in years of bad calls and I'm sorry.

Today felt different.

He left without another word. Jack stayed behind.

And just like that, the space between them started to grow.

Not broken. But no longer whole.

CHAPTER EIGHT –

The bar didn't have a name, just a painted-over sign and two dusty windows that hadn't been clear since Reagan. You didn't find it by accident. You had to know it was there. And Liam knew.

He parked the bike under the flickering streetlight. Stepped inside. The smell hit him first — old wood, spilled beer, and smoke even though smoking was banned years ago.

Behind the bar was **Tommy**, gray beard, eyes sharp, denim vest so worn it looked more like skin. He used to ride. Everyone knew that. No one knew what made him stop. But we've all heard stories.

Liam sat down at the bar.

Tommy poured a glass without asking. Just set it in front of him.

"You look like you've seen too much and said too little," Tommy muttered.

"I need to ask you something," Liam said.

Tommy raised an eyebrow.

"I got this friend," Liam said, "he's... not doing good. We've been through a lot. Started out just trying to get out of a bad place, and now we're deep in something else. I'm not sure I even recognize myself anymore let alone my friend."

Tommy leaned against the bar.

"You trying to save him?"

Liam didn't answer right away. Just stared at the drink.

"I'm trying not to lose him."

Tommy nodded like he'd heard that before. Maybe lived that before

"You ever think maybe he's already lost?"

Liam clenched his jaw.

"Then I'm riding with him. Until the wheels fall off."

Tommy was quiet for a long time. Then he said, "Sometimes staying close to a man in freefall is the only shot he's got at landing on his feet."

Liam looked up.

"I'm not here to save him," he said. "I'm here so he doesn't go down thinking nobody gave a shit."

Tommy poured another.

"You got more loyalty in you than most. But it'll gut you if you let it."

"I know."

Tommy raised his glass.

"Then ride careful. And when the time comes, don't be the one still holding the brakes. Sometimes you gotta bail out."

That night, Liam pulled up to Jack's apartment.

Didn't call. Just knocked.

Jack opened the door, shirtless, scars on his body from God knows what. He looked surprised. Then wary.

"You here to throw more truth at me?"

Liam shook his head.

"I'm here for whatever's next."

Jack stared for a long second.

Then nodded.

"I got a Big one," he said. "Could change everything."

"Then let's go change something."

They didn't hug. Didn't shake hands. Just stood there in the glow of a hallway bulb that buzzed like it might die.

Liam left with a knot in his stomach but a smile on his face.

They were back.

Not because they were okay. But because they weren't going to let each other go down alone.

CHAPTER NINE –

This one felt different.

There was planning. There was structure. Jack had gone quiet again — not the calm-before-the-storm quiet, but the kind that looked like focus. Liam recognized it. It was the same silence Jack wore before fights in high school. Before prison. Before everything broke the first time.

The job was a warehouse — cash drop once a month. Fenced goods, private money, untraceable. Shane brought it in. Said it was clean.

Jack and Liam didn't trust clean jobs anymore. Especially not a clean Shane job.

They brought masks. Gloves. Two-way radios. Rented a van. Jack drew blueprints by hand. Liam scoped the place for three nights. 5 days of tactical training and rehearsal. It was laid out like this:

No alarms. No security. Just two old men counting cash and locking up early.

It was supposed to change everything.

Money to disappear.

Move the families.

Buy time.

Buy peace.

They waited in the alley across from the loading dock. Engine running. Doors half-cracked. Jack loaded the last clip and looked over at Liam.

"You ready?"

Liam nodded but didn't move.

Jack frowned.

"What?"

Liam stared straight ahead.

"If this goes bad," he said, "I want you to walk."

Jack shook his head. "Don't do that."

"I mean it. You run. No weight on your back. No martyr shit. You get to the van and drive until you forget the road back."

Jack looked at him like he didn't know who he was anymore.

"Don't talk like it's already over."

Liam finally turned.

"It's not. But it could be. So just... remember I said it."

Jack nodded once.

Then:

"You're not just my brother. You're the only thing that ever kept me from being the worst version of myself."

Liam's jaw tightened. "Then don't make me regret it."

The job went sideways ninety seconds in.

Shane jumped the gun — didn't wait for the signal. Kicked the door and screamed. One of the old guys had a pistol under the desk. Fired twice.

Liam ducked. Jack moved like he had a sixth sense. Tackled Shane, and dragged him down. One shot hit the wall. One hit flesh.

The second man was on the floor screaming. Liam disarmed him, chest pounding.

Shane was bleeding.

Not bad. But loud.

Too loud.

They loaded the cash fast. Jack took point. Liam drove. Sirens were closer than they should've been. Someone had tripped a silent.

They parked in an underpass twenty minutes later. Shane pale. Cursing. Holding his side.

Jack and Liam stepped away, near the road. Not speaking.

Liam lit a cigarette. Jack took it from him halfway through.

"I saw it in your eyes," Jack said. "You thought about leaving me."

"No," Liam said. "I thought about surviving."

Jack leaned against the concrete wall.

"I don't think I'm built for peace."

Liam turned to him.

"We weren't built for it but we can find it, Jack."

Jack looked at him. Like he wanted to believe it.

Then he said, "If they come for us… I'll handle it."

Liam nodded once.

Then:

"You go down… you go down with your name in my mouth. Every time I ride. Every mile."

Jack didn't smile. Just reached out and bumped his fist.

It was the softest goodbye they'd ever give each other.

They didn't know it then.

But the next time they stood that close…

There'd be bars between them.

CHAPTER TEN –

The shop was quiet that night.

Not silent — the tools still hung in their places, the lights still buzzed, the scent of oil and heat still clung to the air. But there was a different kind of quiet. A final kind. Like the garage knew what was coming.

Jack sat on the stool near Bay Two, rolling a socket in his palm. Liam stood across from him, wiping down the counter even though it was already clean.

Neither of them said it.

They didn't have to.

The cops hadn't come yet, but Jack had made the call. No lawyers. No run. No deals.

He was going to take it all.

Liam knew. He just didn't know how to stop him.

"You sure?" Liam finally asked.

Jack nodded.

"They want someone," he said. "And I've already got the jacket."

Liam clenched his jaw. "You think I can live with that?"

"You'll have to."

Jack didn't say it bitterly. Just stated it. Like a man reading a weather report.

He knew Liam well enough to know he could handle it, whether he liked it or not.

"You always wanted out," he added. "I just bought your ticket."

Liam looked down at the rag in his hand. His knuckles were white.

It took him a moment to calm down. Finally, he scoffed,

"This ain't what I meant."

"I know," Jack said. "But it's what we got."

They stood in it a while longer. The silence. The fear. The love.

"I'm not gonna write," Liam said.

Jack smiled — soft and tired.

"I wouldn't read it if you did."

That made them both laugh. Just a little.

Jack sighed, the kind of sigh that says "Well that's that" he stood. Tossed the socket onto the workbench.

He looked around the garage like it was the last place he'd ever feel free. Then he walked over to Bay Three — the one they always said they'd turn into a teaching bay, a clean slate, something for the future.

He tapped the wall once.

"Make this something," he said. "Don't let it sit."

Liam stepped closer.

"Scouts honor." He joked.

Jack turned. Reached out. They didn't hug. Didn't shake. Just bumped fists.

Then Jack said, almost in a whisper:

"Whatever happens… you cash this new life ticket."

Liam swallowed hard.

"You too."

Jack didn't respond. Just let out a little chuckle as if to say "Yeah right."

Then.

He just walked out.

Didn't look back.

Liam stood in the garage until the morning light started to creep in under the door.

Bay Two stayed empty.

Bay Three stayed waiting.

And Bay One — the one that had always been his — didn't feel like his anymore. In fact that whole garage had changed for him that night.

CHAPTER ELEVEN

It had been three years.

Jack stopped counting after the first. You couldn't keep track of time in a place like this — not without it turning on you. Days didn't pass in here. They wore you down like water on stone.

The tier was always loud. Not from voices, but from the buzz — doors, radios, boots on concrete. Jack moved through it like a ghost. Not the top dog. Not the weak link. Just a man you didn't bump shoulders with unless you had a death wish.

His hair was grayer. Shoulders broader. Eyes colder. His once clean skin was covered by hate and tattoos. Scars acted like his resume, he was tough to kill.

He didn't smile much. Not even when he got letters from Shannon or photos of Liam's kids. He read them slow, stored the details like fuel, and then buried them deep where nothing could get to them.

He had a routine. You needed one.

Wake up before the call. Pushups. Cold water splash. Quiet prayer, even if he didn't believe. Eat. Work detail. Back to the cell. Write. Read. Think. Don't talk unless you have to. Don't feel unless you're alone.

He thought about Liam sometimes. Wondered what kind of dad he was. If the garage still had Bay Two marked off. If the bike still sat untouched. If the shop ever got finished.

Most days, he didn't miss the outside.

But some nights — in the hour before lockdown — he'd sit on the edge of his bunk, elbows on knees, and just breathe. Deep. Slow. Like if he did it right, he'd remember what the air smelled like the night they used to ride the hills.

Like if he tried hard enough, he'd hear Liam's laugh again. The real one. The one that only came out when they were too young to know what they were losing. And some nights he almost did.

On the yard, new kids tried to act tough.

He watched them posture, throw hands, run mouths. He never said a word. But they knew him.

Or at least the stories they've been told about him.

One of them, young, stupid, full of adrenaline, came up to him once.

"You run with the towners?"

Jack didn't answer.

The kid kept going. "I heard you used to ride. Heard you had a brother. That true?"

Jack looked him in the eye.

"I still do."

The kid nodded. Walked away.

And that was that.

In the 3 years Jack had been away Liam worked to make their dream happen. It was a small club, maybe 15-20 guys at most. But they made a name for themselves. Not through violence. Through respect, loyalty, and a take no shit attitude.

He got a visit once every few months. Shannon. Sometimes Riley came, too. Grown up now. Too sharp for her own good.

She didn't ask him dumb questions. Just sat and talked about the world like he still lived in it.

When the buzzer called time, she'd always say the same thing.

"See you soon Uncle J."

And Jack would answer like he meant it.

"Soon."

But the truth was…

he was still back there.

In the garage. In the ride. In the job.

In the version of himself, he left behind.

The inside wouldn't let him move on.

And the world just kept moving without him.

CHAPTER TWELVE –

They didn't play music when they let you out.

No speeches. No handshake. Just a door unlocking and a guard calling your name like it belonged to someone else.

"Jackson Cole. Let's go!"

He stepped forward.

Signed the release form with a pen chained to the desk. Took the plastic bag they handed him — inside, a black T-shirt, worn jeans, old boots, and a wallet with nothing but an ID and a photo folded twice.

The photo was faded now.

Him and Liam. Arms over each other's shoulders. Grease on their shirts. Smiling like time wasn't real yet.

Jack put it back in the wallet and walked out without a word.

The air outside hit different. Too clean. Too open.

The sky was wide — an impossible blue — and it made the ground feel like it might fall away if he looked too long.

Liam was waiting in a truck that had seen better years. Parked on the shoulder like he'd been there a while.

Jack walked over slow.

No words.

It was like he was trying to film this moment and save it to memory. Every step. Every foot closer.

Liam got out of the truck and stepped forward. Gave a nod. Jack returned it.

They didn't hug. Didn't shake.

But Liam reached out and patted the roof of the truck.

"Let's go home."

They drove with the windows down.

No music. Just road.

For a while, neither of them spoke. The tires hummed and the wind pressed through the cab. Jack stared out the window, watching trees blur into nothing.

"You look the same," Liam finally said.

Jack didn't look over.

"I'm not." He said softly.

Neither one of them wanted it to be true but it was, Jack was different, Liam was different. The whole world was different and Jack wasn't prepared.

Shannon had the porch light on when they pulled in. Jessica and the girls came out to meet them.

She came out with a soft smile and a quiet wave. Jack nodded once. She walked over, wrapped her arms around him without asking.

He didn't hug back. But he didn't pull away.

It was the first time Jack had been held since he went away, it was scary and unfamiliar to him.

"Dinner's on the stove," she said. "Jessica Figured you might be tired of trays."

Jack let out a dry breath that might've been a laugh.

Liam's house was small, quiet. A photo of Riley on the mantle. A smell like real food. Jack sat at the table. Liam handed him a plate. Shannon poured water. Jessica called for girls.

They didn't make it a big thing.

Just sat. Ate. Talked about nothing and everything all at the same time.

The only thing Jack said that whole meal was:

"This feels like watching a life I forgot to have."

Liam didn't correct him.

He just passed him the bread and let the silence say the rest.

That night, Jack stood in the doorway of the guest room.

The bed looked too soft. The sheets too white.

He didn't lay down right away. Just sat on the edge. Shoes still on. Hands in his lap.

Freedom didn't feel like what he thought it would.

It felt like walking into someone else's story.

For that night only he sat, breathed deep, tried to remember the smell on the concrete, the stall air of 100 men in one place, stale blood. Just for one night, he wished to be back there. To hear the doors buzz close and lock him away in his own story.

CHAPTER THIRTEEN –

It wasn't raining. It wasn't dark.

No dramatic thunder. No screech of tires or burning rubber. Just a dry road, late sun, and the kind of silence that comes after a good ride.

Jack had borrowed Liam's backup bike. His own wasn't ready. He said he just wanted to stretch it. "See how it feels," he told Shannon.

He kissed her on the cheek, kissed his newborn son, and said he'd be back before dinner.

The engine was smooth, the tires held tight, and the road was open. Jack felt almost human again. Like the space between him and the rest of the world had finally closed. It was just under a year since he got out, it took a while but he found himself again. Or was at least finding himself.

He took a curve near the canyon — one they'd both ridden a thousand times.

But this time, something shifted.

Maybe it was the loose gravel. Maybe his timing was off. Maybe his reflexes weren't what they used to be. Or maybe it was just luck — the kind that runs out quiet.

The back tire slid.

Jack didn't panic.

He corrected once.

Twice.

And then it went. All at once, like a spilled bucket of oil there was no saving it.

The world flipped. Sky. Ground. Sky again.

He hit the guardrail shoulder-first. Metal met bone. He spun around the guard rail like an Olympic gymnast, body rolling and folding like a planned routine. His helmet cracked on the third bounce. The bike slid off into the ravine. Jack didn't. Jack's body lay there. Peaceful. Quiet. Still.

Everything after that was soundless an endless blackness.

Liam got the call just after six.

By the time he and the girls got to the hospital, Shannon was already in the waiting room. Her face was blank. Not crying. Just still.

"They said he's alive," she whispered. "Broken ribs. Concussion. They had to restart his heart once."

Liam sat beside her. Jessica and the girls opposite them.

Didn't say a word.

Just stared at the wall. Hands shaking in his lap.

Penelope was too young to understand exactly what was going on.

Riley knew, she knew it was bad. She had never seen her dad like this before.

Shannon sat in the hospital room longer than anyone. She didn't cry. She didn't scream. She just sat there, hands in her lap, staring at the man she married and wondering if she'd already lost him somewhere along the tracks.

Jack was out for almost 2 weeks.

When he woke, the room was full of soft machines and the smell of antiseptic.

Liam stared at Jack's busted frame, the lines of bruises blooming like something alive under the gauze.

"You always took the hits," Liam said quietly, like he was admitting something shameful. "Every time we got cornered, every time it got bad... you were the one that stood up first."

Jack shifted slightly, a grimace flickering across his battered face, but he stayed silent.

"You said it didn't matter," Liam went on. "You said some of us were built to catch hell so the other could keep running."

His throat closed up but he forced it out:

"I never wanted you to be the one bleeding for me, Jack. I never asked you to be the shield."

Jack opened his mouth, a dry croak scratching out:

"Somebody had to."

He couldn't feel his left side. Couldn't remember what road he was on.

But he remembered the silence. He remembered the feeling just before the crash — like he had finally found something still inside himself. Some sort of acceptance of who he was or maybe what he was. And then it was gone.

CHAPTER FOURTEEN –

It started small.

Jack would forget names. Walk into a room and stand there like he'd lost the reason for it. Shannon brushed it off at first — stress, meds, exhaustion. Liam did too. You come that close to dying, things take a while to settle.

But it didn't settle.

It grew.

Jack would lose time. Not hours, but minutes. He'd repeat stories, retell old rides like they were yesterday. Except they weren't. And sometimes, they weren't even real.

Liam was the first to really notice.

They were working in the garage, sun low, tools spread across the bench. Jack was cleaning a carburetor that didn't need cleaning. Jack asked for a wrench.

"You already tightened that one," Liam said.

Jack looked down at his hands.

"Oh," he said. "Right."

Liam leaned against the doorframe, arms crossed tight like he could hold the world together if he just clenched hard enough.

"You're still you, Jack," Liam said, the lie tasting like rust on his tongue.

Jack shook his head slow, eyes not quite finding Liam's.

"No," Jack said, voice low. "I'm pieces now."

Liam pushed off the wall, dragging a hand down his face, trying to find something to say that didn't feel like handing a loaded gun to a dying man.

"You're just healing," Liam said.

Jack smiled — but it wasn't a real smile.

"You don't glue a man back together after he's been split down the middle. You just hope the wind don't blow him apart before he makes it home."

Another time, Jack called Riley by the wrong name. Twice. Then didn't remember doing it.

One afternoon, Jack pulled Liam aside, eyes heavy.

"I think I'm still in here," he said. "But something's off. Like… I keep losing pieces."

His eyes couldn't hide his fear, it was maybe the first time Liam saw Jack unsure of anything. For as long as they had known each other Jack was never scared never unsure and if he was Liam certainly didn't see it.

Liam didn't know what to say. He wanted to tell him it would pass. That it was just the meds or the trauma.

But he didn't.

Because Jack wasn't soft. And lies didn't help him.

"Alright," Liam said. "Then we hold onto the pieces we still got and fight like hell to keep 'em."

Jack nodded. But his hands were shaking.

Later that week, they were at Jack's for dinner.

Shannon made Jack's favorite. Something simple. Homemade Shepard's pie.

In the middle of the meal, Jack looked up and smiled.

"You think Nico'll make it out next month?"

The room went still.

Shannon's fork froze halfway to her mouth.

Liam looked up slow. "Jack…"

Jack blinked. Looked confused.

"What?"

"Nico's gone," Liam said gently. "Been gone fifteen years now."

Jack stared down at his plate like it had betrayed him. It's like he was trying to find the time between the mashed potatoes and peas. Like if he could look hard enough he might be able to find that time, stab it with a fork, and chew it back up.

"Oh," he said. "Yeah. That's right."

Nobody said anything else. They just finished dinner in silence.

As Liam and Shannon shared glances Jessica tried her hardest to brighten the mood with a smile and an old story.

It wasn't enough. Not for Liam. Not for Shannon. And certainly not for Jack.

That night, Liam stood on the porch with Shannon.

She lit a cigarette. Hands trembling.

Jack stared off into nothingness, Shannon just watched.

"How bad do you think it's gonna get?" she asked.

Liam didn't answer right away.

"I think we're there," he said.

They watched the sky turn black.

And inside, Jack slept without a sound, without a dream. Jack just slept. And Shannon watched.

Not because Shannon had some fear he would die, but because that was the time she could just watch, and dream and imagine Jack. As he was, as she remembered him.

CHAPTER FIFTEEN –

A few days had passed, Jack and Liam were wrenching away as usual. But Jack didn't seem his usual self. He was distant. Looking of into a void no one else could see. Liam dropped onto the stool across from him, elbows on his knees, hands hanging loose.

"You okay?" Liam asked, knowing the answer and hating himself for asking anyway.

Jack didn't look up.

"You ever get tired of carrying a dead man around, Liam?" Jack said, voice so soft it barely stirred the dust in the air.

Liam's chest tightened.

"You're not dead," he said, but it came out a whisper, like maybe even he didn't believe it anymore.

Jack gave a slow, humorless smile.

"Been dead a long time. Just no one had the decency to bury me yet."

Liam shifted forward, like he could reach across the dead air between them.

"We can fix this," Liam said, desperate and breaking. "We always fix it. We ride it out. That's what we do."

Jack finally looked at him — really looked — and it was worse than any blow Liam had ever taken.

"Not this time, brother," Jack said, the words like cracked bone.

"Some rides end in the dirt."

In the stillness of morning Bay Two smelled like old oil and winter dust. Jack opened the shop before the sun was full, he left the door half open,

letting the cold bleed in. The bike he'd wrecked sat crooked in the corner, a ghost of something faster, younger, less broken.

He dragged an old stool under the steel beam overhead. His boots scuffed the concrete once, twice. He tied the rope with the kind of quiet attention he used to save for rebuilding engines — steady hands, no wasted movement.

The shop lights buzzed above him, flickering like tired eyes.

No notes. No calls. No warning.

Jack climbed the stool, set the noose around his neck, and stared out into the garage where he'd spent half his life dreaming about getting out.

About building something bigger than the trackside town that never forgave or forgot.

There was a beat — a long, hard breath — and then he kicked the stool away.

The rope snapped taut. His boots swung once, twice, a twitch, and then stillness. It was a stillness that the shop had never known and wouldn't know after. For that brief second in time, everything was just as it was supposed to be. Still.

Jack and Liam didn't spend every day in the shop. Some days they were together all day. Others they'd leave notes to let the other know they had stopped by. Maybe it was fate or bad luck but Liam was busy that day. And Jack was alone.

Liam knew something was wrong before he even pushed the door open. Jessica had said Jack missed dinner, hadn't called, hadn't answered. That wasn't new. But tonight, the silence felt heavier.

He found the door to Bay Two ajar. The shop reeked of gasoline and cold air.

And there, framed under the old steel beam, Jack hung — still, heavy, gone.

The world didn't spin. It didn't collapse. It just... stopped.

Liam didn't scream. Didn't fall to his knees. He just stood there, one hand gripping the doorway like it might hold him up like it might change what he was seeing.

Bay Two, where they learned to rebuild engines with nothing but busted parts and bad hands, was where Jack decided he couldn't be rebuilt.

Liam stepped forward once, twice, and then stopped. There was nothing left to say. Nothing left to fix. He had every tool a man could want. And nothing in that garage could fix this.

He cut Jack down lay him next to his finished project and walked away.

He turned off the light on the way out.

Jessica had to call the coroner, Liam just couldn't bring himself to say the words. To tell someone it was real. That Jack was gone.

The funeral was small.

Family. A few "out of towners",. Shannon. Liam.

Riley cried. Penelope asked if Uncle Jack was going to come back.

Liam didn't answer. He just knelt beside her and handed her one of Jack's old patches.

She held it like it mattered.

Then Liam finally spoke.

"I think this was always meant for you to have, uncle Jack just didn't tell me right away."

Riley knew Penelope needed it more. She had her memories. Her stories. She could hold on to them forever. Liam knew it too.

That night, Liam walked into the garage alone.

He turned on the light.

Bay One: his.

Bay Three: unfinished.

Bay Two: quiet.

He didn't cry. He didn't speak.

He just reached up, took Jack's helmet down from the wall, and set it on the lift.

Then he sat in Jack's old stool stared at jacks old helmet and whispered to the silence:

"I would've carried you the rest of the way brother."

And the silence whispered back:

I'm sorry

Liam hung the helmet back on the wall. Looked at it for a second.

He turned with heavy eyes. Walked out. And left the light of bay 2 on. Almost in hopes, Jack would stop by.

CHAPTER SIXTEEN –

Grief wasn't loud.

It was quiet.

It was tools left out in the wrong order. Coffee made for two. The second helmet still hanging on the wall. The silence where laughter used to be.

Liam didn't stop riding. He didn't stop wrenching.

He rode more. Built more.

Every Sunday morning, before the sun was fully up, he'd take the old back roads — the ones they used to race, where the trees leaned just a little too close and the wind felt like memory. He never brought music. Never needed it.

Sometimes he'd talk to Jack like he was still there.

Not out loud. Just… in the way his hands moved. In the way, he shifted into third and smashed ahead without thinking. In the way he slowed at the canyon curve where the crash happened, and would imagine what went wrong.

Sometimes, every so often, he'd catch himself looking back to see where Jack was. He was never too far behind.

Penelope asked once why he kept Jack's helmet on the wall.

"Because some things aren't meant to be put away," he said. "They're meant to make us smile to help us remember"

Jessica found him in the garage one night, standing under the same steel beam, staring up like he could still see Jack's boots swinging.

She didn't say anything. She just wrapped her arms around his chest and stayed there, breathing with him, keeping him tethered to the world he hadn't wanted to be part of without his brother.

Shannon still came by. Less now. Jack's son is became a spitting image of him. They never said his name with a question mark. Just with a pause. And sometimes a smile.

Everyone who knew Jack seemed to carry him the same way.

Heavy. But worth it.

In the garage, Liam had started building something new.

Bay Three — the one that sat empty for years — was finally being filled.

A kid from the neighborhood stopped by asking for help fixing a beat-up Harley. Liam said sure. Then another came. And another.

He didn't plan it.

It just happened.

Call it divine intervention.

He didn't call it a business.

Didn't put a sign on the door.

But people came.

Because something about the place felt sacred.

The old-school club members would lend a helping hand every now and again. Life lessons and bike lessons. They were happy to help either way.

It was happening. Their dream was alive.

One night, Liam was locking up. The shop was clean. The air smelled like grease and rain.

He turned off the light and looked back once.

Bay One: his.

Bay Two: untouched, helmet still on the hook.

Bay Three: full of tools and life.

He stood there a while. Soaking it all in. Staring at a dream Jack never got to see.

Then he said it, soft, like a secret:

"We did it."

And in that moment, he swore he could hear a laugh — low, familiar, just behind him — like Jack had never really left.

Because some ghosts don't haunt.

They ride beside you.

Forever.

But forever is a long time to be missing half your heart.

Some nights, after the garage closed and the tools went quiet, Liam would sit in Bay Two, boots on the cold floor, hands empty, breathing alongside the empty air where Jack should have been.

He didn't pray. He didn't scream.

He just stayed.

Because that's what brothers do.

Stay. Even when the road runs out. Even when there's nobody left to hear your engine on the horizon.

Some ghosts didn't haunt you.

They just kept riding with you — in the empty chair, in the empty stall, in the weight you carry across every mile you don't want to ride alone

CHAPTER SEVENTEEN –

In quiet moments Liam would day dream to the past, to simpler times;

It was a summer afternoon — the kind that smelled like dust and sun-baked pavement.

They were thirteen.

Jack had found an old frame behind a junkyard, half-rusted and forgotten. Liam brought the tools. They spent the whole day in the alley behind his mom's house, turning it into something that could move.

It didn't run well.

The throttle stuck, the front tire was bald, and they had to push-start it every time.

But it moved.

They took turns riding it in slow circles, laughing, sweating, high off the idea that they had built something out of nothing.

At one point, Liam killed the engine too hard and nearly toppled over. Jack caught the bars before it hit.

"You're gonna ride us both into the ground," Jack said, grinning.

"Better than never leaving the tracks," Liam shot back.

Jack wiped the sweat from his head and looked at the open street beyond the alley.

"You really think we'll make it out of here?" he asked.

Liam didn't answer right away.

"Don't gotta make it far," he finally said. "Just far enough to feel like we were meant to stay."

Jack nodded. Thought about that a while.

Then he reached into his pocket and pulled out two patches he'd drawn on ripped denim with a Sharpie.

One said: out of

The other said: towners

He handed Liam the one that said towners

"We're not there yet," Jack said. "But someday… this'll mean something."

Liam took it.

"Already does."

Years later, the patch was still hung in Penelope's room.

Framed now.

Old and faded.

Probably the only non-pink thing she owns.

But still holding shape.

Sometimes the younger guys will ask about the past, ask about Jack.

Liam usually tells them the same thing

"Life's meant for enjoying. So enjoy it."

Just like them.

Just like the ride.

Made in the USA
Middletown, DE
07 June 2025

76685763R00056